BROKEN MEMORY

BROKEN MEMORY

A NOVEL OF RWANDA

Élisabeth Combres

TRANSLATED BY Shelley Tanaka

SCHOLASTIC INC.

New York   Toronto   London   Auckland
Sydney   New Delhi   Hong Kong

First published as *La mémoire trouée* by Élisabeth Combres

Design by Michael Solomon.
Cover photograph copyright © Finbarr O'Reilly/Reuters.

Copyright © 2007 by Gallimard Jeunesse.
English translation copyright © 2009 by Shelly Tanaka.
All rights reserved. Published by Scholastic Inc., 557 Broadway, New York, NY 10012,
by arrangement with Groundwood Books.
Printed in the U.S.A.

ISBN-13: 978-0-545-35130-0
ISBN-10: 0-545-35130-8
(meets NASTA specifications)

2 3 4 5 6 7 8 9 10   113   20 19 18 17 16 15 14 13 12 11

The author would like to thank
Le centre régional des lettres de Midi-Pyrénées
for its support.

À Manu
À mes parents
À Fabienne et Christine

"He did not only kill my mother.
He killed humanity."

— *A survivor of the Rwandan genocide*

BAD DREAMS

1.

They are there.

Behind the door.

They are yelling, singing, banging, laughing.

Mama's eyes are wide with fear.

Soon she will be nothing more than suffering on the ground.

Cut up and bleeding.

Then, finally, set free by death.

2.

Emma woke up with a start, exhausted by the same nightmare that she had almost every night. Ever since that day in April 1994, when the men burst into the house and murdered her mother.

She didn't see it happen, but she heard everything, huddled against the wall behind the old sofa, trembling with fear. To keep from screaming, she kept repeating to herself what her mother had ordered when the first blow of a club battered against the door — "Slide behind there, close your eyes, put your hands over your ears. Do not make the slightest move, not the slightest noise. Tell yourself that you are not in this room, that you see nothing, hear nothing, and that everything will soon be over. You must not die, Emma!"

Everything was over quickly after that, just as her mother had promised.

But for Emma the nightmare was just beginning.

She lay curled up in the empty house for a long time, until the ache in her limbs brought her back to reality. She peeled her hands from her ears and very, very slowly opened her eyes.

When she heard nothing but silence, she stood up stiffly and staggered out of her hiding place. She stumbled blindly around the lifeless body of her mother and stepped over the shattered door and through the curtain of rain that blocked the open doorway of the house.

In a daze, she joined the crowds of fleeing families. She slept in the bush, went for long days without eating, drank muddy water from the ditches beside the roads. She managed to dodge the many checkpoints that the murderers had set up to catch anyone who was too tired or careless to avoid them.

Soon she no longer saw many others trying to flee like her. She walked down her road, more and more alone, walking between the dead bodies that blackened the fields and the roads.

Until the day she knocked on the old woman's door.

She had watched her for two days from her hiding place in an empty old chicken coop. Finally, something about the woman's gentle movements made her cast caution aside and approach her.

Sitting on her bed, Emma listened now to the old woman sweeping on the other side of the wall. She got up, pulled on the skirt that lay on the small bench under the window and went to the door of the only bedroom in the house.

When she walked into the other room, the old woman turned toward her, one hand on her waist, the other holding the stiff tuft of straw that she used as a broom. She smiled softly at Emma, then bent over and returned to her work.

After nine years Emma was used to the old woman's silence. She had not said a word that day when she was faced with the terrified little girl asking for something to eat. So that she wouldn't die, the way her mother had told her.

"I must not die," she had whispered in a weak voice, "but I'm hungry. And I am scared, too."

The old woman reacted quickly. Without even thinking, she grabbed the child by the arm and pulled her into the house. Only when the door was closed again did she really consider what she had done.

This thin little girl with the big black eyes, no more than five years old, was one of those who must die.

For weeks the radio had been practically stuttering with rage that all Tutsis must be killed. The old woman was a Hutu peasant, so she was not in danger. But by protecting the little girl, she was condemning herself to death. If the killers found out she had the girl with her, they would both be slaughtered immediately.

So chance had brought them together, in a Rwanda torn apart in terror, fire and blood.

Emma had to hide in the field behind the house several times after that. It was easy to hole up in the mud behind the bank, where the grass had grown quickly since the first rains of April. Meanwhile the men searched, insulted, trampled — they had been told that a young girl was definitely hiding there — then they left.

They came back many times, full of hate and frustration, fraying the old woman's nerves, but they never found anything. The old woman was careful to make sure there wasn't the slightest evidence of Emma's presence.

So she existed without really being there, not really alive and not dead, though she would sometimes feel like a corpse herself, buried in the mud at the foot of the garden.

The old woman and the little girl grew used to each other. When the war ended, they just carried on, and over the years the calm routine of everyday life brought them close. They looked after each other through thick and thin, both simply determined to carry on living. Emma because it was the last wish of her dying mother. The old woman because she never considered doing anything else, not even during the worst moments of her life.

Emma turned toward the cooking area and made herself a bowl of porridge — the same mix of soy flour, sorghum and corn that was fed to babies. She moistened it with milk and swallowed in big spoonfuls. Then she splashed water on her face, washed quickly and set off for the market.

3.

On the road, Emma passed boys and girls her age dressed in their school uniforms — the boys in pale beige, the girls in bright blue. It was time for classes to begin.

"We have to find the money so that you can go to school," the old woman had said to her once. "So that you can be someone later."

But for Emma, "later" meant nothing. Her life revolved around a nightmare. Like a broken record, she kept replaying that horrible night when time stood still. Since then there had been no before and no after. Just the difficult now, where she struggled with ghosts.

She couldn't remember the happy days any more — her aunts, her cousins, the grandfather she loved so much. They were all dead but not buried.

She couldn't even remember the face of her mother, no matter how hard she tried. Sometimes she could see her brightly colored skirt, her outstretched hands, but never her eyes or her smile.

The only thing that remained was that one command: "You must not die, Emma."

So she kept on living. Drifting. Carried by a whirlwind that spun around that night — the night that had taken away her mother and her past.

Two girls jostled against Emma and pulled her out of her daydream with their bright laughter. She sneaked glances at them. They looked alike. They were probably sisters. Their hair was cut short and their blue uniforms were faded, as if they had been worn by several big sisters or cousins who had grown out of them.

Emma looked into the sparkling eyes of the younger girl and suddenly wanted desperately to be like her.

Was it school that made her so happy? She had a hard time imagining herself sitting in a classroom, or even busy learning her lessons in the house in the evenings.

She couldn't even remember the face of her mother. How could she remember anything else? It would be as if someone asked her to bring in the vegetables without having any place to put them that would protect them from the wind, the rain and thieves.

Emma sighed and stared down at the pavement. Then she carried on to the market two kilometers away.

4.

On Sundays the old woman got ready for mass. Emma never went with her. She couldn't understand about this God that people sang to in church. It was in those same churches that men, women and children had been beaten senseless, shot, hacked up, burned dead or alive.

How could everyone have forgotten all that? Had the entire country lost its memory?

"I'm going to see my husband after mass," the old woman whispered, without looking up or waiting for an answer.

Emma left the house an hour after Mukecuru. Grandmother. That was what she had chosen to call her back in 1994, a few days after she arrived at the house.

This Sunday, as usual, Emma dressed up, too,

putting on her white blouse and her nicest skirt. She almost smiled when she saw how her brown hand looked against the pale fabric splashed with green, orange and red. She thought she almost looked pretty, even though her body was beginning to feel like more and more of a burden. As a little girl she had been quietly invisible, but a few months ago she had turned thirteen, and now she was as tall as a woman.

She had seen the big change in how men looked at her, especially when she dressed like this. But it was important. It was for the visit. She never missed one.

She left the house, strolled down the dusty path, then turned onto the paved road. You didn't see many cars here, but the giant eucalyptus trees rustled like a crowd dressed up in their Sunday best.

Emma didn't like being out after mass. She ran into too many people. She was relieved when she finally reached the turnoff and practically ran down the grassy path that was almost hidden from the road.

A bit farther on, she slowed down. She didn't

want to get there too early. It was Mukecuru's visit. Emma knew that Mukecuru didn't mind her coming, but she still couldn't get rid of the awkward feeling that she was in the way.

When she reached the end of the path, she was reassured to see the old woman in her usual spot, sitting on the rocky bench in the middle of the clearing. In front of her, wildflowers covered a mound about the length of a man — the grave of her husband. He had died thirty years ago and had been buried in the family compound. Not long after, his sister took charge of the property and chased Mukecuru away.

Today nothing was left of the house but ruins of dried earth worn down by rain and overrun by tall grasses. Only the grave remained, thanks to the old woman who dressed up and came every Sunday to look after it.

Emma sat quietly a short distance away. She liked to come to this place that took Mukecuru back to her past, back to the years when she lived with her husband.

For Emma, such a thing was impossible. Her mother and the rest of her murdered family had never been buried. She didn't even know where their bodies were.

In Rwanda, they said that when the dead were not buried, their spirits stayed around to haunt the living. They became the *abazimu*, the bad spirits — sometimes even bad for those close to them.

Emma looked up when Mukecuru walked in front of her. She looked relaxed and peaceful, as if she were surrounded by people close to her. Emma could imagine them smiling and floating around the old woman.

"That's why she's always so calm," Emma said to herself. "She's never alone. They are there, watching over her memories.

"They *are* her memory," she decided as she stood up. Then she fell in behind Mukecuru, staying a few paces back, and followed her home.

5.

The following Tuesday, Emma went to the market to sell fruit for a woman who worked in a shop and was looking for people to help her make a little extra on the side.

On the way there she noticed the strange boy, the one with the dented head. He was wandering around the way he did every day at this time of year, wearing rags spattered with mud, his head bent, his arms glued to his sides and his fists pressed to his stomach. As if he was holding himself together, afraid of seeing his body fall apart in pieces.

Emma had heard the rumors about him. He was a Tutsi like her. In 1994, he had lived in the west, near Kibuye, on the shore of the big Lake Kivu. His parents and their close friends had joined the rebels of Bisesero — families who, with nothing more to lose, refused to die like animals and had come together to fight back. But the rebels were suffering heavy losses, and one day the little boy was captured.

They said it was a blow from a machete that had dented his head. They also said that the killers had amused themselves terrorizing him, beating him and torturing him before they decided to make him sing.

His life in exchange for information about the rebels.

Emma had no trouble imagining it. She couldn't remember happy times, but cruel moments seemed to come to her easily. She could see every gruesome detail — his cheeks smeared with blood and tears, practically out of his mind, his mouth twisted in fear, fits of vomiting from the stench of the excrement that ran down his legs.

The little boy ended up talking. He told them what he knew about where the resistance was hiding. The others howled with satisfaction and one of them struck him with the machete one last time, thinking that would finish him off.

Emma wondered if he knew how many men,

women and children had died because of what he had said.

Then she shook her head. She had enough nightmares of her own. She cringed and quickened her step.

The young boy saw her looking at him. He saw the way she hurried off. But he no longer expected anything from her or from any of the others. He bent over to pick up a crushed fruit that a vendor had dropped, then moved away while he sucked on the bits of red-veined yellow pulp clinging to the dried-up skin.

Emma was relieved to see the market — the women bustling about in the aisles, their colorful long skirts, the babies on their backs, other children clinging to their legs. Bananas, sweet potatoes, peanuts, passionfruit, cassava and beans blossomed on the mats lying on the ground, were passed from hand to hand, were tossed into the baskets on the heads of the traveling vendors. Customers tested, weighed, discussed, hesitated, then decided to pay. Money exchanged hands quickly, disappearing into pockets, bags or the folds of a skirt.

Emma found the daily bustle comforting. It was as if this group of women, the whole swaying, living mass of the market, took her by the hand and led her, thought for her, decided for her. Everything was simple. All she had to do was give in to it, just go through the same motions that thousands of women had gone through before her.

She pushed into the crush of people, determined to sell her bags of fruit. She clutched her bags and closed her eyes and allowed herself to be swallowed up by the crowd and to forget about her own troubles for one tiny sweet second.

6.

"They are coming, Emma," Mukecuru said, her voice almost a whisper.

They were sitting behind the house on the bench of dried earth, a big black pot full of cassava roots between them.

"Who?" asked Emma. She continued to peel the knobby roots with deft, practiced movements.

"The ones who did the killing in '94."

Emma froze. The knife slid from her hand, clattering against the metal handle of the red bucket at her feet, where she was piling the peeled vegetables.

The old woman moved the pot and the bucket, slid closer to Emma and put her hand on her shoulder. Emma was trembling from head to foot.

"To be judged," the old woman said softly. "Soon they will hold a gacaca court here, the way it was done in the past in the villages. After mass."

"Why here?" Emma gasped, her jaw tense.

"So they can be identified by their victims."

"But their victims are dead!" Emma's voice rose. She slumped down. The trembling stopped. "And the ones who survived, they might as well be dead, too," she added weakly, not caring whether Mukecuru heard her.

The old woman folded Emma in her arms, held her close and rocked her gently.

7.

"Hey, little one. Over here."

Emma looked back, saw the woman turned in her direction and headed toward her, holding out the small bag of fruit that she hadn't yet sold. She'd done well that morning and she was in a good mood, so she didn't notice how angry the woman was until it was too late.

The woman leaned over without even glancing at the bag of fruit dangling in Emma's hand.

"They say you live with an old Hutu," she said, her voice low and threatening. "What are you doing with her? She's one of them, one of the assassins. Don't you know that?"

Emma struggled to answer.

"She…she saved my life," she mumbled, but that seemed to provoke the woman even more.

"And who's to say she wasn't denouncing others at the same time she was hiding you?" she went on, her voice raised. "It happened often."

Emma flinched and said nothing, but that just made the woman angrier. She grabbed her arm and held her still.

"Be careful, girl," she said, her voice low once again. "Look around. The murderers have come back."

Locked together, they both looked at the prison truck that was carrying a handful of men dressed in pink. After the genocide, the prisoners had chosen this color to replace the black clothing that used to be required in the country's jails.

Suddenly the woman, herself a survivor of the genocide like Emma, was wrenched back to her own horrible memories. Clutching Emma's arm, she froze, torn between wanting to comfort her and wanting to shake her a little harder. But now, even in her anger, she was surprised to find herself just as shaken as the frightened young girl.

Emma felt this sudden change in the woman's look and body language. She wrestled out of her grip and ran away.

Without even noticing, she stumbled past the boy with the dented head, who had been watching the scene from a distance. Finally she started to walk, gasping for breath, her body shaking with dry sobs.

She was just approaching the outskirts of town when the truck full of prisoners drew alongside and passed her. The tarp had been pulled up at the back, revealing the men inside.

Three of them were talking, and one voice in particular stood out. Emma didn't recognize it at first, but she felt an uneasy murmur rising around her, a mix of blows, insults and laughs.

It was when she heard her mother scream that she recognized the voice of the man.

A sharp pain cut through her chest. She tried to run, but she was suddenly horribly dizzy, and her legs wouldn't move.

Later, when the truck was far away and she could no longer hear the voice, her uneasiness grew. The real world faded around her as the roar of the assassins, their blows, the pain of her mother and her own terror took shape.

Then, just as she had done that night, she

took shelter against a nearby wall, crouching down and burying her head in her arms.

A few women tried to lift her up, children poked her to make her react. But it was no use.

So little by little, life carried on around her, and her huddled figure eventually blended into the peaceful countryside at the end of an ordinary day.

8.

"Where were you?" Emma could see the question in Mukecuru's eyes when she pushed open the door the next morning. But the old woman said nothing. She knew from Emma's body language and the desperate look on her face that this was no time for questions. She busied herself in front of the stove in the corner, then placed a bowl of porridge on the table.

Emma sat down and looked at her breakfast. She finally started to eat, slowly bringing the spoon to her mouth while she fidgeted with a torn corner of the plastic cloth that was glued to the old chipboard tabletop.

Mukecuru sat down on the other side of the battered table and began to peel sweet potatoes.

Emma stared at the dark hands of the old

peasant woman. Her eyes followed every sinew, the bulging tendons of her arms, the pointy bones of her fists.

Then, leaving her spoon beside her barely touched bowl, she picked up a knife to help Mukecuru and let herself, too, be ruled by her hands.

And she thought about what had happened that morning.

When she finally came to, the boy with the dented head was sitting beside her, leaning against the wall. He was staring blankly straight ahead, so she was able to watch him for a moment. He had fine features and his skin, though covered with grime, appeared to be fairer than her own.

But he heard her stir. He glanced down at her — she noticed his eyes, bloodshot as if they were infected by some strange illness.

Then he got to his feet and headed off without a word.

Emma thought about calling him back, but she didn't know what to say. She sat up, leaned against the wall and watched him disappear down the road, his footsteps gradually growing fainter.

Then she tried to remember what had happened.

She could only recall bits and pieces: the market, the angry woman, the noise of the truck, and then…nothing. Or rather, yes, being overcome by gut-wrenching pain and a tremendous blackness that made her legs buckle. She also remembered the shelter of the wall against her back. That's where she fell asleep.

Later, on her way back to the house, she wondered about that strange boy and the amazing thing he had done. He must have found her and sat down to watch over her, probably when the sun began to set, when the shadows became threatening.

Emma shivered just thinking about spending that night outside.

"You're trembling." Mukecuru's voice brought her back to the kitchen table.

Emma smiled. She cared so much for this gentle woman who knew how to read her silences, who just with her voice and a few words made her feel cared for each day. All that didn't protect her from the nightmares or the ghosts, but it did make her feel stronger and more able to face them.

"Thank you, Mukecuru," Emma whispered, picking up another sweet potato.

A peaceful silence settled over the house, scarcely broken by the sound of knives scraping the vegetable skins.

As the morning passed and a pile of white, naked potatoes grew between the two women, the air became heavy and humid. Gray clouds swept over the horizon and darkened the windows that looked out onto Mukecuru's garden. The light lowered as if it were dusk.

Then the sky split open and heavy rain beat down on the house with a tremendous roar. The old woman and the girl raised their eyes with the same calm movement. They looked at each other for a brief moment without stopping their work.

Then Mukecuru lowered her eyes, and Emma did the same.

9.

Emma slept a lot during the days that followed. On several occasions — sometimes in broad daylight, sometimes in the middle of the night — she would begin to tremble, her eyes filled with terror and her mouth open in a silent scream.

Sometimes Mukecuru stopped her from going to the market. She kept her busy as best as she could, gave her simple tasks to do, and quietly remained close by.

Those empty days were filled with nightmares, but in the end Emma recovered. She didn't remember much, but for a long time she felt a strange, heavy sensation in her limbs and a numb feeling deep in her bones.

KEEPING WATCH

What had he said that had upset the boy so much? What words had he used, she wondered, remembering the silent movement of his lips.

Emma knew that she, too, troubled Ndoli deeply. That night he had spent at her side had opened something up in him, had somehow broken through the fog of his existence. When that truck passed and she fainted, he had recognized the demons that were so similar to the ones that haunted his own days and nights.

At first he kept his distance, watching the women trying to revive her, stopping himself from chasing after the kids who pestered her. Then, when her outstretched body no longer interested anyone, he went over to her, sat down and did not move until morning.

At dawn, he had seen the same old man who had approached him today. The man had watched them for a long time before going on his way without saying a word. And now he had reappeared just when Ndoli was dreaming under the tree, waiting for time to stop…

"Bloody old man," muttered Ndoli and, as Emma watched him from the window, he walked away, his steps unsteady.

11.

That night Emma had her usual nightmare. The next morning, still lying in bed, she tried to remember the face of her mother. She saw her long shadow bending over her, but a dark, shifting mass blurred her face.

Emma's belly clenched. The more time passed, the more her memory seemed to betray her.

She beat her fists against her stomach, curled up into a ball and sank into the old mattress.

12.

Ndoli was gone for a long time. He came to see Emma again one morning in June.

She saw the surprised look on Mukecuru's face as she glanced out the little window. Curious, Emma went over and saw the young boy planted under the tree as if he had never left. He just stood there, not moving, but something had changed. He didn't look as stiff.

"It's his clothes. They're clean now," Emma said to herself.

Every year, he gradually returned to reality as the anniversary of the genocide faded. Those days of commemoration, darkened by the April rains, were filled with the buried memories of another storm. A storm drenched in the blood and agony of a million deaths. The country lived according to the rhythm of the official memorial and the testimonies shared during long night-time vigils, while the rainy season brought torrential downpours, and mud flooded the roads.

"They say we must not forget. I guess that's true," thought Emma as she continued to watch Ndoli. "Mukecuru says the same thing, even though no one remembers how brave she was and even though they still don't trust her just because she is a Hutu. Dear Mukecuru, how ignorant they are," she declared, smiling up at the little window.

Like many survivors of 1994, Emma found it hard getting through the month of April — a time when she was more deeply in the grip of her horrific memories.

For Ndoli it was the same thing, she realized, and now he was better because April was long past.

But something else was different, too. Something that she could not quite put her finger on.

When Emma returned from the market the next day, Ndoli was stationed under the tree once again. She was surprised to see him wearing his school uniform. Usually he didn't put it on until August or September after wandering restlessly for long months.

She walked past him, was tempted to say something, hesitated, felt ridiculous. What could she say to him today? His uniform was from a world she knew nothing about.

She turned away from the big tree and hurried into the house. As Mukecuru looked on, worried, she silently put her money on the table and retreated to the bedroom.

"Tonight," she replied. "Let's finish the day's work first."

Almost relieved, Emma grabbed the basket that the old woman held out to her and obediently went to the chicken coop to gather eggs.

That night, Mukecuru kept her word. She sat Emma down beside her and told her what she knew. She spoke softly and took long pauses between each sentence.

The old woman told Emma that the president had been assassinated, his plane shot down. She told her how the radio had called on people to murder the Tutsis, who were nothing more than cockroaches, and how the whites had left the country. About the roadblocks where the military and the militias checked people's identity cards to decide who would be killed. How a part of the population had gone mad with killing.

Then Mukecuru told her about the Tutsi rebels who came over from Uganda. She told her about the horrible crimes, the looting, the people who grew rich off those who had died or who had fled, about the chaos of a war where no one, neither Hutu nor Tutsi, was safe from the militias, the military, the rebels or even their own neighbors. She told her how the rebels eventually defeated the army, causing thousands upon thousands of Hutus to flee. And that by the end of the war the country had become a graveyard, losing a million of its people.

When the old woman finally stopped, exhausted, her face was hollow, and her eyes had dark rings under them. Emma had taken in every sentence of her gory story.

"So it was the whole country that did the killing."

"No, Emma, there were men and women who did not participate in the massacres, and good people who saved lives. Some of them are dead."

"You were one of them, Mukecuru," Emma said to herself. She leaned her head against the old woman's knee, and Mukecuru softly began to hum one of Emma's favorite lullabies.

15.

The next day when Emma came home from the market, she heard people talking in the house. She slowed down, quietly approached the open window and leaned against the wall.

She recognized the clear, strangely thin voice of the old man who had approached Ndoli.

"I can help her. You must convince her to come and see me."

"She'll have to choose for herself. I won't tell her to do anything," Mukecuru replied in the firm tone that she only used with strangers. On the other side of the wall, Emma smiled, thinking how gentle Mukecuru was when she spoke to her.

"Tell her about me," the old man said. "Tell

her where she can find me. Then she can be the one to decide."

The old woman hesitated.

"Can you get rid of her nightmares?" she asked.

His voice softened.

"I can try. Talk to her."

Silence filled the room again. Emma didn't see Mukecuru, but she could just imagine her standing there, determined and still as a statue, studying the old man.

"I'll talk to her," she said finally, in a tone that signaled the conversation was over.

Emma hurried behind the house and waited until the visitor was a long way off. When she came back, Mukecuru was still standing in front of the door, staring at the road.

"You were here," she said without looking at Emma.

"He's a strange old man," Emma answered, leaning against the wall. "He chases away nightmares…?"

She smiled, looking at Mukecuru. The old woman hesitated briefly, then turned and smiled back.

"You can find him at the medical clinic behind the church," she said as she went back into the house.

16.

"He killed my sister!" the young woman said, pointing a trembling finger at the prisoner who was silently facing his accuser.

They were standing in the middle of a small crowd. About a hundred people were at the gacaca, sitting in a semicircle in a grassy clearing dotted with patches of brown. A number of them were angry at the woman.

At the edge of the circle, other men wearing pink were waiting for their turn, leaning against a tree or sitting cross-legged, some of them with their backs turned. Others looked down at the ground. All of them wore blank, hollow expressions.

"She's lying!" a woman screamed from the audience. "She saw nothing, she was hiding. Otherwise she'd be dead, too!"

Watching the scene from a distance, Emma began to tremble, as if the accusation had been aimed at her. She identified with the woman who had come to testify. When she heard that a gacaca was going to be held that morning, she decided to go, but she had not found the courage to join the crowd.

She listened to the young woman go on with her story, encouraged by the judges sitting behind two tables that had been placed side by side. Among them was an old white-haired man, a former teacher; a woman of about fifty who was in charge of the medical clinic; and a young man Emma didn't know, elegant in his pale suit.

The young Tutsi woman said she had heard her sister's murderer bragging about his crime. He'd gone back to his house after his "work day" — that's what the people who killed during the working day called it — carrying his machete as if he'd just been working in the fields.

That day of massacres had ended, like many others, with a party, with beer and grilled meat. There was always plenty of meat, since the murderers would slaughter the herds of their victims.

The young woman admitted she had been hiding, but this man was the neighbor of her parents. He had watched her and her sister grow up.

There was no possible mistake. It was his voice she'd heard.

The crowd grew angrier as her testimony became more detailed. Unable to take any more, Emma stood up to leave.

That's when she noticed that Ndoli was slightly below her, also watching the scene from a distance.

To stay out of sight she quickly sat back down, more heavily than she meant to.

The boy heard her and turned around. He hesitated for a moment, then waved shyly. Emma took a risk and smiled back. He looked surprised. Then he moved away from the grumbling crowd in the clearing and made his way up the hill.

When he reached her, she made a place for him on the carpet of dried grass.

They both felt awkward. They didn't know what to say, so they turned their attention to the trial.

A young Hutu boy, a little older than Ndoli

— maybe eighteen or nineteen — had replaced the previous prisoner.

"They still hate us," Emma said in a whisper.

"Maybe…because they feel guilty," Ndoli stammered.

Below them, the young Hutu was being defended by a genocide survivor in her forties. She confirmed that he had beaten her father in April 1994, but made it clear that he had done it while he was being threatened by the members of the Interhamwe militia. They were the ones who had waved their blood-spattered machetes and forced him to kill her father, a sick old man. Maybe they were trying to make the boy one of them. That first crime often led to others.

The woman added that she didn't understand why she was not dead as well. The attackers had left, claiming that they were finished for the day, but that they would get her, too, just wait.

Of course, she did not wait.

The young prisoner told his version next. It was similar to the woman's story.

Emma turned toward Ndoli. She could feel him becoming more tense. His jaw was rigid and he clenched his fists as the teenager, who would have been scarcely ten years old at the time of the genocide, described his crime and his ordeal.

The young Hutu's story had things in common with Ndoli's, but his weakness had not led to the loss of his own family. He probably stood a good chance of being recognized as a victim by the gacaca, and officially pardoned in everyone's eyes.

Ndoli knew that would never happen to him.

Emma saw that he was upset, and she didn't know how to comfort him. But she knew she had to say or do something. After all, he hadn't hesitated when she had blacked out on the side of the road that time.

Suddenly the gacaca seemed a million miles away, as she realized that their first real encounter was about to end in disaster. She stopped second guessing herself, and ended up saying the simplest thing in the world.

"Thank you for the other night."

Caught off guard, Ndoli looked at Emma, and all at once his eyes filled with tears. To stop herself from crying, she gave him a big fake smile, crinkling her eyes and showing all her teeth.

The cheerful look on her face was so unexpected that Ndoli felt something let go deep inside him. He started to laugh, even though he was still crying. Then he wiped his face, took a breath and shrugged his shoulders, as if to excuse himself for being so pitiful.

17.

"This boy is fragile," Mukecuru said when Emma told her what had happened. "Take care with him, Emma," she warned.

Emma didn't understand. She thought the old woman was being unkind to Ndoli, just like the whole world was against him, she told herself bitterly. It wasn't fair. He was a victim himself. He was doing the best he could.

But Mukecuru's words would come back to her a few months later. She would understand what she meant then.

18.

Emma and Ndoli met each other often after the gacaca. She told him about the gossip at the market, and he reported on what was happening at school — both passing on news about what was going on in their separate worlds. She would put down the women who had made fun of them. He told her about the funny, cruel and often disappointing things that went on at school.

Emma liked one of his stories in particular. It was about a girl at school who had fought to join the boys' soccer game at recess, even though they didn't want her to, and she ended up playing so well that she caught the attention of the coach of a girls' team.

Emma often asked Ndoli about this girl. She became sort of an imaginary friend, the kind you secretly admire and who makes you want to do better yourself.

"I would like to be like her," she confessed one day. "But I could never do that."

"How do you know? You've never set foot in a school," Ndoli replied, a little annoyed. He had exaggerated the accomplishments of this girl to a certain degree, and Emma's huge interest in her was starting to irritate him.

That evening, Emma thought about what Ndoli had said. She hadn't paid much attention at the time, in spite of his unusually gruff tone. But now, stretched out under the big tree, she dared to dream.

How did she really know what she could or could not do? She began to imagine a life for herself as a daring schoolgirl caught up in a thousand and one activities, in a recess without end.

19.

Ndoli lay on his stomach beside Emma, in the grass behind the low wall that surrounded the schoolyard. He didn't hesitate for a second when she asked him to take her to watch the recess break. He had run out of true or even almost true stories, and his imagination was seriously beginning to fail him when he tried to think up new ones.

"When are they going to come out?" asked Emma without taking her eyes off the empty yard on the other side of the wall. She was trembling with excitement, her forehead glued to the dry stones, her hands on either side of the gap in the wall that allowed her to see without being seen.

The students burst onto the playground

before Ndoli could answer. He watched Emma. He was only interested in recess because she was. She drew back when she saw the sea of children pouring out the doors of the big yellow building, but quickly went back to her observation post.

The students swarmed into the yard, the striking contrast of their blue and beige uniforms making it easy to tell the girls from the boys, even from a distance.

Ndoli chose a hole of his own — the old wall was full of them — and pointed out the students he had told her about. She was surprised at how ordinary the girl soccer player looked. She was walking with another girl that Ndoli had never mentioned, and she didn't look like the heroine Emma had imagined.

She was just about to tell Ndoli how disappointed she was when she noticed a student walking toward them. Small and dirty, he snuffled and dragged his feet. One leg of his shorts was torn and spotted with blood. Standing near the wall, he passed his sleeve under his nose. Then he found a clean tissue and wiped the traces of snot from his cheek.

His finger to his lips, Ndoli grabbed Emma's wrist and pulled her away. They lay on their backs, their heads leaning against a solid section of the wall. The boy was right on the other side. He sniffed loudly and spat on the ground. Then he began to kick the stone wall violently. Emma and Ndoli could hear him taking out his frustration.

Suddenly, a whistle rang out, making Emma jump. Ndoli burst out laughing and the boy stopped, his foot suspended in midair. Then, either because he realized someone was spying on him or because he was afraid of being late, he took off, getting his legs tangled up and tripping in mid stride.

Ndoli was sorry to see Emma leave him to take up her observation post again in time to watch the students rush back into their classes. Behind them the dust fell in slow motion, cloaking the yard in silence.

"Who was that?" Emma asked, sitting down in the grass facing the wall.

"Kanuma," Ndoli answered, sitting down beside her.

"The one who's always being blamed for everything?"

"Yes."

Ndoli started to get up, but Emma continued. "Why don't the others like him?"

"I don't know."

"And you?"

"What about me?" Ndoli said hesitantly.

"Do you like him well enough?"

"No."

"Why?"

Ndoli hugged his knees and briefly touched the scar on his forehead.

"He's weak," he said abruptly, without looking at Emma. "He doesn't stand up for himself. That makes the others meaner. Whatever happens to him is his own fault."

"Why would you…" Emma started to say weakly.

Why would you say such a thing, she finished to herself.

Flustered, Ndoli got up. Emma stayed sitting.

"And me, how would I be if I was in the schoolyard?" she asked suddenly, while Ndoli, not knowing whether he wanted to leave or stay, wandered aimlessly around her.

He stopped, taken aback. Then he sat down again with his back to her. She leaned against him.

"Tell me!" she demanded.

"I don't know," he answered slowly. Then, surprised by his own meanness, he added, "I don't see you at school."

"Oh, I see…" Emma murmured unhappily. She straightened up so that she was no longer touching him. "So I don't belong at school?"

He panicked, not knowing what to say. Finally he leaned back timidly until he felt her back again. She stiffened at first and he froze. Then she leaned against him. He remained rigid, afraid that she would move away again.

She began to rock her shoulders lightly from side to side. He rolled his muscles against hers, raised his head and silently thanked the trees.

Emma turned around suddenly, put her arms around Ndoli's shoulders and kissed him noisily on the cheek. Then she got up and left him sitting in front of the low wall.

THE RETURN

20.

Emma came around the side of the building that housed the clinic and headed toward the reception area. The door was always open.

A little girl was sitting sideways on an oversized chair, swinging her legs back and forth, her eyes locked on a map of Rwanda that was tacked to the opposite wall. The other walls were covered with posters. One showed a mother nursing, another a baby sleeping beneath a mosquito net, and a third portrayed a smiling couple beside a couple sick with AIDS.

Two women were having a lively discussion across a small desk. One of them was holding a paper that she kept trying to show the other woman.

Rooted to the spot in the doorway, Emma

was reminding herself why she had come, when the old man appeared.

"Hello, Emma. I'm glad you came."

He looked impressive in his light-colored suit. For some reason she thought that he must be very strong.

He was beside her in two strides, placed his hands on her shoulders and whispered, "Everything is going to be all right, I promise you."

The old man led her into his office. She sat down on a metal chair, gray like almost everything else in the room. He sat facing her, their knees almost touching. When she stiffened, he smiled, shifted his chair back and leaned toward her.

That's when she noticed the hollow and the funny bump at the base of his skull. She quickly lowered her eyes, clasped her hands together and wondered once again why she had come.

But the old man was right. Everything was okay. He talked a lot. As for Emma, she didn't say another word after she asked him where he was and what he had done in 1994.

Ndoli had told her that the old man had suffered as much as ten men. He convinced her that she could talk to him because he was one of the survivors of the genocide.

Then Emma talked to Mukecuru, and that had finally made up her mind.

"I believe he's a good man," the old woman said. "Listen to him at first. Watch him closely. See whether he deserves your trust. You're the only one who can decide."

On the way back from the clinic, Emma thought about the old man's story. His life had been unbelievable. He had survived the many massacres that the Tutsis had suffered. In 1963 they hunted him down; in 1973 they cut his throat, treated him, then hunted him down again; in 1990 they put him in prison and tortured him; in 1991 he was beaten before he managed to get away and hide; in 1994 he was captured and left for dead. All because he was a Tutsi. Now he was scarred but still standing, his dignity intact.

Unlike Ndoli, he was able to hold his head high…

Emma was shocked that she would even think this. She had no right to compare the actions of a man with those of a seven-year-old child in the hands of cold-blooded killers. She was torn as she thought about how Ndoli's life was at a standstill. She felt tenderness, then pity, then guilt for having come out of it better than he had. And in the end she felt ashamed of the feelings that Ndoli had stirred up in her.

For the rest of the day she tried not to think about her own past. Then at dusk she took her place beneath the big tree and tried to remember the face of her mother. But she couldn't. Mostly she just heard a muffled noise, murmured cries. The bark at her back became as smooth as a wall and she could feel her body shutting down.

To pull herself out of it, she raised her head and fixed her eyes on the front of the house, the windows lit up like bright stains on a heavy black curtain. She squinted to make sense of this strange sight, noticed the door, then the little window where she used to spy on Ndoli.

Only then did she manage to struggle to her feet and run into the shelter of the house.

Out of breath, she slammed the door and threw herself against it. Her heart was beating so hard she could hear the ground and the walls quiver.

In the room, Mukecuru startled. Outside the night was black and haunted.

21.

Emma went back to see the old man many times. She became used to his gray office. She noticed new little things each time she visited, as if her eyes were just learning how to see. She especially liked the drawings hanging on the wall in a cluttered corner behind a stack of files that seemed to be waiting to be put away. Every time she looked at the drawings, she had an urge to tug on one of the deeply buried files, just to watch the old papers fly apart and scatter on the floor.

Ever since their second meeting, the old man had been trying to make her tell him her story. But the words wouldn't come. Emma retraced her life with Mukecuru, but she couldn't go back any farther.

So he asked her to draw her past instead.

"Happy or sad events, Emma. Whatever you want," he said reassuringly.

"I don't know how to draw."

He insisted, showed her the clumsy drawings that other children had hung on the wall to prove that anyone could pick up a pencil and express themselves. She could see houses and smiling people.

Then Emma remembered a drawing that she had noticed on her way into the office that day. It was not on display but was waiting to be filed in a drawer.

It showed a man with two pointy boots hanging from a square body. He had a rifle instead of an arm and it was aimed at a child with huge eyes in a blank face with no mouth on top of a vertical line without arms or feet. A fountain of red spurted from the head of the child and dripped down to the bottom of the page.

Emma could just see the blood running off the page and over the edge of the desk to form a bright red pool on the floor.

That's when she grabbed a fistful of pencils.

It was her turn to try to tell her story.

She tried to draw her mother, fought to show her eyes and her smile, but she could only make crude curves and stupid circles. Her mind refused to remember this face, and trying to draw it changed nothing.

She ended up pushing away the papers and pencils as she settled back in her chair, trembling and hating herself.

Then the old man calmly asked her if she wanted to try once more to tell him about her life before the genocide.

She managed to murmur only a few sentences from the far side of the desk, but she stopped trembling.

During the sessions that followed, Emma made progress. She remembered her grandfather and his mean wife, then took the pencils and drew her father the way she imagined him.

She smiled the whole time she drew him, and her drawing joined the others on the wall above the stack of old files.

22.

Then the day came when the old man asked Emma to draw her most terrible memory.

She tried again and again.

She always began by drawing a vertical line to represent the wall that she had huddled against. But that's as far as she got, scratching out and blackening the short line over and over, her fingers clenched, wearing down the tip of the pencil.

"I can't draw the voices, the beating, the crying. I didn't see anything," she said one day, discouraged and exhausted. "I can't do it."

The old man did a strange thing then. He walked over to her, tilted his head to one side, and whispered in a low voice, as if he were telling her a secret, "So pretend you are the sofa, and try to tell me what you see. You're in no danger. You're just a sofa."

Emma's eyes widened. What an idea…

After a few moments of hesitation, she hid her face in her hands and tried. She wasn't able to turn herself into a sofa, but she found herself transported back to the scene, more like a piece of the ceiling, perfectly harmless.

And she let the voices, the beating, the crying come back, and she pictured the crime in her head.

What she saw was unbearable. Her breathing speeded up, then stopped. She thought she was about to drown when the old man's voice broke into her nightmare.

"Tell me what you see, Emma. Don't keep it to yourself."

She managed to let go a little, took a deep breath, plunged back into the scene and described the horror. It felt so unbelievably real.

When she came back to the old man, it was as if she had been sleeping standing up. He walked over to her, his hands on her shoulders, his eyes full of compassion.

"It's over, Emma."

23.

"You wanted to know," the old woman said.

Emma just stood there, frowning nervously.

She was supposed to return to her home village — her mother's village — to get a document that would prove that she had in fact been her mother's daughter, thus a Tutsi and a survivor of the genocide. Then she would be entitled to money that the state had set aside for the surviving victims — money that would allow them to look after themselves and have better lives. And, for the many children and teenagers who had been on their own since the massacres — most of them desperately poor orphans — it would allow them to enroll in school.

Emma wasn't yet sure she wanted to go to school, but Ndoli's stories and their tense conversation behind the wall had made her want to be with young people her own age.

She looked at Mukecuru. She did want to know where her mother came from and to see the house where they had lived before everything was lost in her broken memory.

But the journey scared her. She was afraid of going back to the place where her life had stopped. If she was right there, the ghosts would be even stronger than they were in her bad dreams.

"You'll find your missing memories there," the old woman added. She knew how frightened Emma was.

The girl sat on the little bench, her safe spot in a dark corner of the room.

"I'll go," she whispered. "I'll go soon."

She slid her hands between her knees, her eyes fixed on the ground. Then she rocked back and forth, as if she were calming a baby.

24.

The house where she had been born was about sixty kilometers from the old woman's place. And it was many long months after her talk with Mukecuru before Emma set off along this road for the second time. Back in 1994, she had fled on foot, hiding in fields, sleeping in the bush, nibbling on rotten fruit every few days, drinking dirty water whenever she could.

This new journey, ten years later, would be very different.

Before she left, she told Ndoli about her plan. He wanted to go with her, to protect her, he said. But she told him no. She wanted to face her past and get her life back on her own. Besides, the month of April was approaching, the time when she always noticed the first signs of his dark madness returning. She was already uneasy about this trip. She would not be able to be strong enough for both of them.

One day when she was feeling discouraged and exhausted and refused to spend time with him, he grew impatient, even angry.

She could see that he was shattered by her rejection. His eyes glazed over, his jaw became rigid, and he staggered off as if he were drunk.

Emma felt badly, too. She had a nagging feeling that she was punishing Ndoli, that she had abandoned him. During a long sleepless night, she tossed and turned, upset that she had hurt him so much.

He was her only friend. Without him she would probably still be battling nightmares.

The next morning, she decided to leave right away, even though she was upset and exhausted, and Mukecuru suggested that she rest for one more day.

It was only when she was on her way that Emma remembered the old woman warning her about Ndoli's fragility and about being careful with the power she had over him.

25.

Emma couldn't relax until the outskirts of town were far behind her. Only then did she look up and pay attention to the men, women and children who were walking with her on the side of the road. She was surprised at how free and easy it felt to be anonymous. For the first time ever, it felt good to be surrounded by people, walking with them or past them, invisible in the crowd.

Most of her traveling companions were peasants who walked this same road every day. A few were on bicycles harnessed up like horses. It was funny to see men gripping the handlebars, their rear ends in the air as they fought to pedal to the top of a long hill. Some of them gave up and walked up the steeper hills instead, but they still struggled to push their bikes that were weighed down with huge bulging white sacks of grain that looked heavier than a pile of anvils.

From time to time, the sounds of an old beat-up motorcycle would pierce the silence, belching, farting and hissing wildly. Every once in a while a vehicle surged around the bend — the powerful four-by-fours of the aid workers or white tourists, luxurious black sedans with tinted windows belonging to some important person from the capital, a broken-down van driven by a storekeeper in the village, a minibus or crowded coach running between Kigali and Butare, Rwanda's other big city.

Emma liked to watch the way the women would calmly shift aside toward the trees when a car passed, gracefully swinging the colorful umbrellas that protected them from the sun. She shuddered at the unruly schoolchildren who waited until the last second before getting out of the way of the huge engines spewing out oil.

Then the engine noises would gradually disappear and peace would return to the roadside. And Emma would turn her attention back to the people she passed, trying to imagine what their dreams were like, what their lives were like.

She overheard a heated conversation between two teenaged boys lying in the grass, their heads leaning against the pavement. They wanted to become soldiers just like an older brother and a cousin who had been recruited by the rebels during the genocide.

She was touched by the sight of a tiny boy, his forehead creased in concentration as he struggled to keep up with the brisk pace of his mother while he hauled a yellow oil can that was as big as he was.

After several hours of walking, she decided to take a minibus. She reluctantly handed a few Rwandan francs to the driver, then slid into a spot between two travelers. Her shoulders, her arms, her back, her thighs, her entire body were squeezed in close, unsettling contact with her neighbors. Their clothes rubbed together and their sweat mingled. For a while she put all her energy into holding herself stiff, afraid she would never get out of that hellish box. But in the end she just gave up.

Once she relaxed, she was able to sneak glances at the people smiling around her. She saw how a sort of good mood was developing among the travelers, in spite of their complaints about the driver or the occasional rowdy passenger.

There was a big, tough-faced lad who she thought looked mean, until she watched him place his hand on the head of a baby swaddled on the back of its mother so that it wouldn't be crushed by the sliding doors. She admired an elegant woman until she saw her rudely scold a crippled old man who was trying to sit down to rest his legs.

Emma realized that every thing and every person had an outside and an inside, and that the two were not necessarily the same.

She also saw how beautiful her country was. After one of her fellow passengers got off the bus she was able to lean against a window. The countryside unfurled before her eyes like a patchwork of luminous greens stretching into the distance — the cultivated slopes of valleys irrigated by rainwater. As far as she could see, hills poked into the sky, nudging aside the clouds. From time to time little houses popped up like tiny brown islands in a sea of banana groves with their large bright green leaves.

Emma realized just how little she knew about her own country and how inexperienced she was. At the beginning of the journey, she had been ready for anything to happen, especially the worst. She never imagined she would be surprised by so much, feel so carefree. She could see no signs of the past horror, no scars. She saw nothing on the faces around her that reminded her of the tragedy she had lived through and that had shaped the entire country.

This journey showed her a Rwanda that seemed to be at peace.

She could see things with a positive frame of mind — places and people that had looked blacker than hell to her ten years ago.

And for the first time, she felt strong enough to face the future, as uncertain as it was.

26.

A second minibus took Emma to her village.

By the time she arrived, the energy she had gained during her journey was draining away as fast as the fading daylight. At the small open-air bus depot, travelers were rushing to get home. Some were met by friends and relatives, others by persistent taxi drivers. Those less well-off were leaving on foot or heading toward the mobilettes and bicycles waiting for clients on the side of the road. Emma saw several with loads of luggage precariously balanced on their narrow racks.

Before long she was the only one left. Afraid that she would never find the courage to finish her journey, she looked around and just started to walk. She passed the old cars that had been abandoned behind the shack that housed the ticket office.

When she reached the edge of the depot, she stopped again. She felt the night deepen, saw the red earth of the road in front of her turning brown.

She placed her small blue-and-black backpack on the ground and searched through one of the pockets, pulling out a piece of paper and carefully unfolding it. Mukecuru had written down the name of the woman she was supposed to stay with overnight. Emma didn't know how to read very well — the old woman had taught her only the basics, which was all she knew herself — but she knew enough to get by.

Small shops surrounded the open-air terminal, so she headed toward one that was lit up — a grocer's with telephone service according to the symbols on the sign — and asked a man sitting in front of the door for directions.

He looked tired, his eyes dull, a bitter wrinkle running from the corner of his mouth where his pipe was wedged. He barely looked alive.

"He's not old, though," Emma thought. She

tried to imagine what kind of a life he had led, but she was in a bleak mood. She imagined him in 1994, decided he was a torturer at first, then a victim, a survivor without family who had come out of it well, judging by the grocery store. No matter what, he had still ended up with dull eyes, tired features and a bitter mouth.

The man slowly dragged twice on his pipe, held it in his left hand and without a word pointed it toward the house she was looking for.

27.

Emma had never seen a house so full of things. In the salon, the furniture seemed to be fighting for space. Embroidered and crocheted white doilies smothered every armchair, bureau and table. The walls were scattered with religious pictures to cover up cracks in the plaster.

Emma had a hard time concentrating as the woman welcomed her. Her attention kept shifting between the doilies that threatened to slide off the sofa where she was sitting and the sheer fabric of her hostess's blouse, which seemed to be struggling to contain a powerful and generous bosom.

"The button is going to pop off," Emma thought, distracted by so much luxury.

Everything here was the exact opposite of

Mukecuru and the life she led. Yet she had recommended this woman, whose name she had been given by a neighbor who knew her family.

She welcomed Emma warmly.

"I knew your mother, you know. We went to the same school. We never talked to each other much, because she was younger than me. But I remember her well. She was very smart. It caused a lot of jealousy. However, I believe she only wanted the same thing all us Tutsi students wanted back in those days. She wanted to get by without being noticed. There weren't a lot of us in the school. Only the best and some of the privileged had the right to go to school."

Emma forgot about the doilies and the blouse and tried to imagine her mother as a child. What kind of a little girl was she? Had she looked like her mother when she was six years old, ten, thirteen? Would she be like her when she was twenty or twenty-four? Had her mother been twenty-four? She didn't even know how old she was when she died.

"Would you like a Fanta?" the woman repeated, touching Emma's arm lightly.

"Um…yes…thank you," she babbled. She smiled at the sight of the low-cut sea blue neckline right in front of her nose.

Her hostess took the smile as being aimed at herself, and she smiled back.

"I stayed away a long time," she went on, as she took the cap off the lemonade. "I went to work with my aunt, who left the country for Kinshasa in 1973. We came back after the end of the war in 1994 like most of the exiled Tutsis. We'd at least been tolerated there before the war, but after the victory of the FPR, we had to get out fast. But I'm boring you with my stories. You're falling asleep. Tomorrow, if you like, I can show you your house."

"Is someone living there?" Emma asked, awkwardly trying to pull herself out of the sofa while she tried to replace the doilies that she had rolled into a ball on her knees without even noticing.

"Oh, no. It's nothing but a ruin now."

28.

The next day Emma went through the necessary formalities to get the document that proved that she really was the daughter of Pacifique, a young Tutsi woman murdered during the genocide at the age of twenty-two.

After that she found out how to get to her house. She went alone and had no trouble finding it. It lay in ruins below the main road on a hill overlooking the valley.

Emma had escaped right after her mother's murderers left. She didn't know whether the killers had returned to destroy the house and finish their work, or whether looters had come by later. Whatever had happened, they had gone at it with a vengeance. And time had done the rest. Ten years had passed.

She walked down toward the ruin. She was both dreading and hoping to uncover her buried memories. Had she really once been four years old and living here with her beloved mother?

She looked at the rubble, circled the trees, scanned the horizon, the hills. Then she ran her hands over the stones and took off her sandals so she could walk in the grass in her bare feet.

Her eyes, her hands, the soles of her feet — would they be able to remember?

She walked around for a long time before she dared to turn her attention to the inside of the crumbling house, though she knew she would not find her mother's body there. After the genocide the dead had been gathered and taken to an official memorial to the victims.

Emma tried to concentrate, but she couldn't think straight.

Coming here had been a mistake. This place was so familiar and yet completely strange at the same time. She couldn't get hold of it, couldn't get hold of her past. She couldn't find the courage to walk into the ruins. She was too afraid of stirring up the old nightmares.

But before she gave up and left, she tried one last time, casting her eyes over the rocks piled inside the entrance to the house.

She suddenly noticed a piece of blue plastic inside the roofless walls. She hesitated for a moment, then carefully placed one foot on the rubble and tugged on the tarpaulin.

It wouldn't budge. It was bigger than it looked.

Finally throwing caution to the wind, Emma crouched down and frantically started to clear away earth and stones until she managed to lift up the old plastic. Underneath was a small pile of books weathered by the damp.

The girl sat down, stared at the old books, then timidly brushed her finger over the faded covers. Her heart raced. All this had belonged to her mother…

Feeling bolder, she grabbed a book that was larger than the others, the soft cover bending between her fingers.

Her slender brown hands turned the illustrated pages, and suddenly, she was there. Holding her breath, Emma raised her eyes and, for the first time in ten years, she saw her mother bending over her, her eyes filled with an unanswered question.

When she came to her senses, her cheeks were covered with tears. In each hand she was holding a piece of the big book, which had fallen apart under the pressure. She glanced at the pages scattered on the ground, then at the ones she was clutching in her hands.

That's when she noticed the photograph pinned under her right thumb. The paper had yellowed, the edges were frayed. Emma saw the questioning eyes of her mother and smiled back weakly.

Her search was over.

Exhausted, she lay down on the ground. She had finally managed to rebuild the walls of the ruined house where she had been born, and where her mother had died. The murderers had failed to crush her memory.

"Mama," she murmured. "Mama," she repeated more loudly, laughing and crying at the same time.

Emma was still lying in the middle of the rubble when night fell — so suddenly, it was as if someone had turned off the light. She turned onto her side and fell fast asleep, her damp cheek glued to the faded photo.

EPILOGUE
Ten Years Later

That journey changed Emma, and under the watchful gaze of her mother she continued to grow stronger. When she returned to Mukecuru's, she enrolled in school, and after spending several years studying beside much younger classmates, she became a teacher.

Today she is twenty-four years old. She lives in her parents' house, which has been rebuilt to look exactly the way it used to. She was able to find her mother's remains in the memorial dedicated to the genocide victims and had her buried in the garden overlooking the valley. She devotes all her energy to her work, but whenever she can, she spends long hours near the gravesite.

She is now at peace with her past, and she looks to the future with confidence.

Ndoli has continued to see the old man. Things are getting better now that he understands that he was not responsible for the deaths of his relatives, and that he should not feel guilty for surviving them.

But every year Emma spends the first two weeks of April with him, on the anniversary of the genocide — a time when the country remembers and the young man is once again racked by nightmares.

Mukecuru died after Emma received her diploma, knowing that the young woman would now be able to manage without her.

The old man continued to work with the child survivors of 1994. Now he sees many children orphaned by AIDS. He encourages some of them to go to school, as he did with Ndoli and Emma.

He also spends a great deal of time testifying about the genocide, to build a bridge between the victims of this unspeakable tragedy and the rest of the world, and to help the survivors find their way back into the human community.

AUTHOR'S NOTE

This book is a work of fiction. The people and places described in it are inspired by the real Rwanda as I experienced it, but they are imaginary.

But the historical context is absolutely real.

Rwanda is a small country in central Africa. Its 10.3 million inhabitants are divided into three groups: Hutu, Tutsi and Twa. Before the 1994 genocide, Hutus made up 91.1 percent of the population and Tutsis 8.4 percent. Today the census does not identify people by these groups.

Between 1899 and 1950, Rwanda was colonized by the Germans, then the Belgians.

Traditionally, to be Hutu or Tutsi was similar

to having a social status linked to an activity such as agriculture or raising livestock. The colonizers solidified these societal groups by associating them with ethnic groups and issuing identity cards, thus increasing tension between the populations. They began by favoring the Tutsis, who were at the top of the social scale. Then, with the coming of decolonization, they facilitated the taking of power by the majority Hutus.

In 1961, a Hutu government was elected and declared themselves opposed to "Tutsi domination." As the government rapidly slid into dictatorship, it began to practice anti-Tutsi discrimination and commit large-scale massacres. Subsequent governments continued to commit the same crimes, making violence against the Tutsis commonplace for four decades. In 1994 the conditions were in place to carry out the worst crime of all — the genocide of the Tutsis.

The extermination of the Tutsis, which involved close to a million deaths, began the night of April 6, 1994, after the assassination of Rwandan president Juvénal Habyarimana. The massacres were aimed primarily at the Tutsis, but also at Hutus who were opposed to the government in power. They were committed by the Rwandan army and by militias, with the complicity of the local authorities and certain members of the Catholic church. Villagers killed their neighbors, encouraged by the official media promoting hatred against the Tutsis. It was the rebels — sons and grandsons of the Tutsis who had been exiled from Rwanda since the 1950s, who brought an end to the genocide in July 1994 by defeating the Rwandan army.

As for the international community, it did not intervene to prevent or stop the genocide. An operation led by the French army was put in place at the end of June 1994, but it continues to be the subject of heated controversy. The gray areas that remain revolve around the role and intentions of France toward Rwanda, before and during the genocide.

Rwanda continues to rebuild, but the tensions between the populations have not disappeared. Inspired by traditional village tribunals, gacaca (ga-cha-cha) courts have been set up. Though not perfect, they have allowed more than a million cases involving crimes committed by men, women and children during the genocide to move through the justice system. The perpetrators of the most serious crimes have been referred to Rwanda's regular justice system, and the organizers of the genocide appear before the International Criminal Tribunal for Rwanda set up by the United Nations in Arusha, Tanzania.

ACKNOWLEDGMENTS

This book would not have seen the light of day without the cooperation of all those who agreed to respond to my questions, tell me about their lives, explain their work, guide me, talk to me about everything and nothing…

A big thanks to the young Rwandan genocide survivors who shared their stories and to those who allowed me to meet with them, especially Gasana Ndoba; to the professionals who spoke to me about the trauma suffered by child survivors and their difficult search for identity, Célestin Sebuhoro and Jean Damascène Ndayambaje in particular; to all those who, in Brussels, Kigali and Paris, shared their knowledge and explained their views about Rwanda; to Jacqueline Uwimana and Gaspard Kalinganire for their warm welcome, our long discussions and sharing with me on a daily basis.

Special thanks to Pierre Vincke and Janouk Bélanger from RCN Justice et Démocratie, for their excellent contacts.

ABOUT THE AUTHOR

A former journalist, **Élisabeth Combres** has worked as a reporter in France, Latin America and Africa. She began writing for young people after working as editor-in-chief for the magazine *Mikado*. She is the author of several children's non-fiction titles, including *Mondes Rebelles Junior*, winner of the Prix Sorcières in 2002. In 2004 she collected the accounts of adolescent survivors, psychologists and humanitarian aid workers to use as the basis for this book, her first novel. Originally published in French, *Broken Memory* was selected for the Prix NRP (Nouvelle Revue Pédagogique) and the Prix des lycéens allemands. Élisabeth lives in Grenoble, France.